Captive

A Comedy in Two Acts

by Jan Buttram

A SAMUEL FRENCH ACTING EDITION

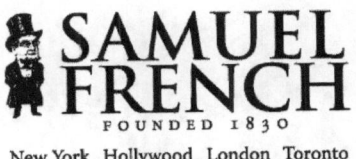

SAMUEL FRENCH

FOUNDED 1830

New York Hollywood London Toronto

SAMUELFRENCH.COM

ISBN   978-0-573-69358-8   Printed   in   U.S.A.   #5876

CHARACTERS

GORDON POUND — 83, the father
SALLY POUND — 35, the daughter
CLAY POUND — 40, the son

TIME & PLACE

Summer, 1983
Rural East Texas

Captive was presented by the Pulse Ensemble Theatre, Alexa Kelly, Artistic Director. It was directed by Celine Havard and had the following cast (in order of appearance).

SALLY POUND............. Laurie Sanders-Smith
GORDON POUND .... David Clarke
CLAY POUND .... Steve Deighan

Costume Design: Fran Cole
Lighting Design: Patti White
Properties: Karen Wimmer
Set Design & Construction: Paul Trapani, The Company
Sound Design: M. Donovan
Production Coordinator: Marc Raphael
Associate Producer: Kate Fitzgerald
Stage Manager: Bill King

Captive was winner of the Playwright's Award at the American Folk Theater, Inc., NYC and was originally presented at New Plays Series at La Mama.

The set is a den/kitchen combination (if necessary, the set can consist of the den only, with the kitchen adjacent off stage) in a comfortable, modest farm house in East Texas with large screened windows upstage. There are two exits. One to a hallway leading to the rest of the house. The other is an outside entrance. There are several chairs, a kitchen table, icebox, a couch, a desk and a television. At curtain, it is very early morning. The voice of SALLY POUND, 35, is heard from outside. SHE is trying to get in the house.

SALLY. What is this? A joke? Who locked the door? This is the country for Christsake, you don't lock doors.

(The sound of a CAT screaming is heard.)

SALLY. Jesus Christ! Miss Kitty, I'm sorry! *(Calling, coaxing.)* Here, kitty, kitty, kitty. Come here! *(Pause.)* Ok, forget it ... bitch. *(Shaking the door.)* Goddammit. *(Window screen shakes.)* They locked the door and left the windows open ... perfect.

(SALLY wrenches the screen off the window. SHE begins climbing into the room. SHE has one leg in when the SHADOW of a man carrying a shotgun is seen approaching cautiously. HE aims the shotgun at Sally. GORDON POUND, 83, speaks:)

GORDON. Whoever you are, hold it right there and state your business!

SALLY. (*Freezes in mid-air.*) Holy shit! Hold it a second! (*Pause.*) Dad? Is that you? What are you doing here?

GORDON. You move a muscle in the wrong direction and I'll blow your head clean off.

SALLY. I'm not moving.

GORDON. Now, what are you doing climbing in my window?

SALLY. Dad, it's Sally.

GORDON. Who do you want?

SALLY. Sally Pound, your daughter?

GORDON. She ain't here.

SALLY. Yes, she is here. Dad. I'm her, I'm Sally, it's me. (*Pause.*) Dad? If you don't believe me, turn on a light.

GORDON. Put down your gun!

SALLY. What gun? It's a beer can.

GORDON. I never knew Sally to be a drinker.

SALLY. Jesus, don't you recognize my voice?

GORDON. I ain't heard from Sally in a while. Might not recognize her voice if I was to hear it.

SALLY. Dad, please put the goddamn shotgun down and turn on a light.

(*Pause.*)

GORDON. I'll turn on the light. But I ain't putting down my shotgun.

*(GORDON switches on a lamp. We see SALLY holding a
can of beer in one hand. SHE is pretty, dressed in blue
jeans and T-shirt.)*

GORDON. What in the tarnation are you doing
crawling in the window?

SALLY. *(Drinking her beer.)* It was open.

GORDON. Could have got yourself killed. One more
second and you'd have been dead.

SALLY. Isn't Jack here?

GORDON. He's gone.

SALLY. He didn't wait for me?

GORDON. I guess not.

SALLY. Thanks, brother. Aren't you suppose to be on
a vacation?

GORDON. Didn't go.

SALLY. Did Mother go?

GORDON. She dern sure did.

SALLY. I'm surprised you'd let Maude go on vacation
by herself.

GORDON. Couldn't talk her out of it.

SALLY. You two have never been apart for a day.

GORDON. I would have had to hear tell of it until my
dying day if she had to miss seeing where Jesus walked and
talked. She should be over in Iran by now.

SALLY. Dad, I think it's Israel.

GORDON. That's what I said, Israel. *(GORDON
surveys the window screen.)* Dern your hide, you busted
my screen out.

SALLY. Sorry.

GORDON. If you don't prop her up, we'll have flies all
over the house by daylight.

SALLY. First light, I'll nail it back.

GORDON. (*Insistent.*) I'd appreciate it if you'd fix it *now*.

SALLY. Alright already! (*Pause.*) Have you got a small hammer?

GORDON. No.

SALLY. You haven't got a hammer?

GORDON. I ain't got no small hammer.

SALLY. No hammer at all?

GORDON. I've got a regular-sized hammer ... but that's not what you asked for—you asked for a *small* hammer.

SALLY. My mistake. Might I use the regular size hammer, please ...

GORDON. (*Agitated.*) The hammer is in the tool shed but there's nary a light out there. I wish you'd do like I say and just prop her up.

(SALLY polishes off her beer, sets it down and exits outside. SHE begins trying to put the screen back in the window talking to her father from OFF.)

GORDON. You ain't ever going to get her back going at it that way.

SALLY. Give me a chance, Dad. (*The window screen falls to the ground.*) Ow, sweet Jesus, I broke my toe. Ouch!

GORDON. Ought not to have taken her down.

SALLY. I'm very sorry I did. (*After a pause, SALLY begins again.*) So, it's good to see you, Dad.

GORDON. What are you doing here?

SALLY. I came to see you!

GORDON. Dern! I don't believe that ... you didn't even know I was here.

SALLY. I'm on vacation.

GORDON. You've got to have a job before you can take a vacation. I wasn't under the impression that you worked at anything.

SALLY. (*Referring to the window.*) How does that look?

GORDON. She's low at the top.

SALLY. What?

GORDON. You got her on crooked.

SALLY. All right ... (*The screen moves.*) Is that better?

GORDON. Yep. Now it is. (*Pause.*) You drove here from New York City?

SALLY. All the way.

GORDON. (*Picking up her empty beer can.*) Drinking and driving—that's a good way to get yourself killed.

SALLY. I plan on camping out with you for a few hours, if you don't mind the company.

GORDON. You're by yourself?

SALLY. Yep. (*SHE bangs the screen into place with her boot.*)

GORDON. What are you using for a hammer?

SALLY. My bare fist.

GORDON. The devil.

SALLY. (*Crawls back through the window and latches the screen from the inside.*) So, my question is *why* didn't you go on this vacation with Mother?

(*Pause.*)

GORDON. I had me a car accident.

SALLY. You did?
GORDON. Yep.
SALLY. Dad? Are you alright?
GORDON. Yep. But Maude ain't got a car anymore. I just got a little bump on the head. That's all it was, but Doc Reeves didn't want me going on a long trip. Wanted to watch me. I told him I'd been watching myself for eighty-two years, don't think I need him to do it for me.

(SALLY exits without GORDON realizing it. HE continues talking to the air.)

GORDON. Well, it don't bother me one bit Maude took off by herself. She can dern well do what she pleases. Always has and always will. I have no earthly desire to visit a foreign country. This dern vacation was Maude's idea. She's talked about it for years. How she wished she could go to the Holy Lands and make a scrapbook of the visit. The preacher got a cut rate for him and the Sunday School class ... Only reason I was going was to protect Maude. Thelma Ferris wound up going in my place. I can't stand to be around Thelma Ferris.

(GORDON realizes he is talking to himself. HE turns on the kitchen light and peers at a clock. SALLY enters from outside carrying a knapsack and an ice chest.)

GORDON. Not very interested in what I've got to say, are you?
SALLY. I was getting my stuff.
GORDON. Dern, I didn't aim to go to Iran and that was that.

SALLY. Well ... whatever.

GORDON. (*Looks at the clock closely.*) What does that clock say?

SALLY. Five o'clock.

GORDON. Lord a mercy!

SALLY. Best time to travel. No traffic.

GORDON. Well, I'm going back to bed.

SALLY. So, I missed Jack?

GORDON. He left you a note somewhere on Maude's desk.

SALLY. Well, Christ, Dad ... why didn't you say so?

GORDON. I'm telling you now. Goodnight! (*GORDON begins to exit.*)

SALLY. Sorry I scared you.

GORDON. Be time to get up before long.

(*GORDON exits. SALLY goes to the kitchen table and picks up an envelope. Opens it, takes out a note and shakes the envelope to find something more.*)

SALLY. (*Reading the note.*) Great. *Clay* has it. That's a joke. (*Draining the last of her beer, SALLY walks around the room, unsteadily. SHE goes to the ice chest, opens it, stares inside for a moment, pulls out another beer. Gets her knapsack, begins searching, pouring everything out on the kitchen table. SHE searches her jean pockets, pulling out two crumpled dollar bills and change.*) Two dollars and fifty cents ... (*SALLY searches again, finds and chases down a pill with a large swig of beer. SHE picks up the phone, dials and waits.*) Yes, I want to leave a message. Hi, Jack, you brain-damaged alcoholic fuck! You are suppose to be here to meet me! All I find is a note saying Clay is going to give me money. *Clay*? I might as well take out a loan with the CIA. I hate Clay and he hates me! Did you remember that? Well? (*SHE slams down the phone, moves the ice chest in front of the couch and falls across the couch, exhausted.*)

(*The LIGHTS brighten to morning with sounds of BIRDS singing, a ROOSTER crowing and a COFFEE POT beginning to perk.*
GORDON enters the room dressed in overalls and a work shirt. HE stops for a moment to view the covered body on the couch.)

GORDON. Can't get up to go to bed. (*GORDON stares out the window for a moment, reading the temperature from a thermometer hanging outside, HE rubs his eyes and tries it again. Takes his glasses off, wipes them and tries again.*) Already eighty-five. (*GORDON stops to look at the ice chest, picks up several pieces of clothing strung out on the floor, and drops them on Sally's covered body. HE goes to the kitchen, pours himself a cup of coffee and takes a series of pills. HE drops one on the floor—gets on hands and knees searching the floor and finds it.*) And I'm tired of taking all these dang pills.

(*GORDON sits down and turns on the RADIO searching for the farm news. A low VOICE is heard giving the price of hay, tomatoes, corn and announcing the upcoming auctions, particularly the Texas International Brahman Bull Sale. HE pours a bowl of cornflakes with milk when the PHONE rings. HE answers phone.*)

GORDON. Hello. No. She ain't here. She's on vacation. You'll have to make do with me. (*Pause.*) Well, of course she's alright. Why wouldn't she be? (*Pause.*) My night wasn't too good. How was yours? (*Pause.*) Well, take another dose of it. Yeah. If you don't feel good, I'd take another dose. If I was you, which I'm glad I ain't, I'd quit smoking them dern cigarettes. You're too old to be smoking. Maude made me quit forty years ago and I'm dern glad she did, even if she did complain of cigarette ashes on her floors for two years after there weren't none. (*Pause.*) You're going to blow yourself up with that oxygen you use when you can't breathe. They'd be picking up pieces of you all over Bowie County. (*Pause.*) I'm hanging up the phone if you cuss me! Can't talk any longer because my Post Toasties are sogging up. (*GORDON hangs up the phone.*) I don't need to know if that woman got through the night alive. Dern, if she didn't, there's nothing I can do about it. Buy her a coffin. (*HE tastes his cereal, spits it back in the bowl.*) Soggy.

(*GORDON looks at his watch. HE rises wearily, pours out his cereal, wipes down the table top then pulls a vacuum cleaner out of the closet. HE plugs the electric cord into the wall. It starts with a wild ROARING SOUND. SALLY jumps up from the couch.*)

GORDON. What's the matter? You look as if you'd seen a ghost ...
SALLY. (*Grabs a quilt and drapes it around her and quickly crawls back onto the couch.*) God, I was dreaming ... I had just crossed the Arkansas state line right smack over the German border. The sentries stopped me. I was

surrounded by Gestapo dressed in cowboy boots and Stetson hats ... Clay was the leader, he made me stand in a ditch, aimed a 30-30 at my head, I heard the click ...

(The PHONE rings.)

GORDON. Can't get nothing accomplished this morning. Clean up that mess.

SALLY. What mess?

GORDON. The mess you left lying around. And answer the dern phone.

SALLY. Turn off the vacuum cleaner!

GORDON. *(Switches the cleaner off, and answers the phone.)* Hello!

SALLY. What is that thing ... a Hoover torture chamber?

GORDON. What in tarnation? Yeah, she's here. Just a second. It's your brother.

SALLY. *(Jumps to the phone.)* Hello? Clay? Surprise! Yeah. Jack told you what was up? *(Pause.)* Yeah. Dad's fine. *(Pause.)* Great! It'll be good to see you. I really appreciate this, Clay. I wouldn't ask unless it was absolutely necessary ... *(SALLY hangs up.)* Clay is coming over.

(Pause.)

GORDON. Be fine by me if he stayed over at his house. *(Pause.)* Haven't I told you not to drive alone late at night?

SALLY. I ... probably, you have told me.

GORDON. But you don't pay any attention to me, do you?

SALLY. Something like that.

GORDON. Where's that boy?

SALLY. Jack?

GORDON. No.

SALLY. Clay?

GORDON. Dern, no. Not your brothers. (*Pause.*) I can't think of his name. Dagblasted ... you know the one I mean ... that one you married.

SALLY. *Don* is in New York.

GORDON. Are you sure?

SALLY. (*Teasing.*) I know where my husband is, do you know where your wife is?

GORDON. Ain't got the slightest idea.

SALLY. I'm one up on you. (*SALLY falls back onto the couch.*)

GORDON. If you're going to sleep more, go to your bedroom.

SALLY. Dad, just let me lie here for a few minutes.

GORDON. Dern. (*Pause.*) Mother makes me vacuum this spot every morning because it's where everyone walks and if you don't get the dirt up, people track it into the rug. (*GORDON turns on the cleaner. HE yells over it.*) It'll just take a second. (*GORDON vacuums for a few seconds but stops agitated.*) I wish you'd get off that couch and go into the bedroom.

SALLY. You aren't bothering me.

GORDON. But you're bothering me.

SALLY. This is insane!

(SALLY exits, wrapping her comforter around her in a fury. GORDON continues speaking, not realizing she has left the room.)

GORDON. I guess you ain't never heard of people having car trouble? They's lots that are never heard of again after they get themselves stranded on the highway. Someone just slits their throat from ear to ear with a pocket knife and throws the body in a ditch somewhere. I wouldn't want to die like that. Bleed to death on the dern highway.

(SALLY re-enters dressed in cutoffs. HE turns off the cleaner.)

GORDON. I do believe Clay Pound is the surliest individual I ever did meet. Both your brothers are on the serious side. Then there's you.
SALLY. Yep. Then there's me. How about a cup of coffee?
GORDON. You got a quarter?
SALLY. Can you change a twenty?
GORDON. Help yourself, but leave me my second cup.

(SALLY pours herself a cup of coffee. SHE leisurely opens the refrigerator door and peers inside. SHE stands contemplating.)

GORDON. You're letting all the cold air out.
SALLY. What?
GORDON. What are you looking for?
SALLY. I'm not sure.

GORDON. Want butter for toast?

SALLY. No.

GORDON. Milk?

SALLY. No.

GORDON. Then don't stand there looking in the icebox. You decide what you want before you open the refrigerator. You don't stand holding the door open until you decide what you want.

SALLY. Nevermind. (*Mumbling.*) Now I remember why I don't come home.

GORDON. What?

SALLY. I said, it's good to be home.

GORDON. If you want something, I'll fix it for you. Mother doesn't like you in her kitchen.

SALLY. Coffee is fine.

GORDON. Then, close the dern door.

SALLY. (*Slamming the door shut.*) It's closed. May I finish the vacuuming for you?

GORDON. I'm finished. (*GORDON begins storing his vacuum cleaner.*)

SALLY. (*Incredulous.*) That was it?

GORDON. All it needs.

SALLY. Sweet Jesus, I could have stayed on the couch.

GORDON. The couch is not a place for a person to sleep. Maybe a nap ... I take a nap there every afternoon and sometimes in the morning if I'm not feeling good.

SALLY. And how are you feeling today, Dad?

GORDON. Same as I felt yesterday. You irritate me worse than that dern Jack. He'll go grocery shopping with me and put anything he wants into my cart. That Diet Coke is expensive. (*Pause.*) Well, it's time for my morning news. I better warm her up. (*GORDON turns on the TV.*)

SALLY. The TV is a woman?

GORDON. What's that?

SALLY. The television ... you said warm *her* up ... your television is a woman?

GORDON. Ain't everything a woman?

SALLY. Then you ought to get her checked out, her face is red as a beet and her grass is blue.

GORDON. Looks fine to me.

(*GORDON goes to the ice chest. As HE begins to lift the lid, SALLY stops him.*)

SALLY. What are you doing with that, Dad?

GORDON. Seeing if you got any food in here that will ruin.

SALLY. Leave it alone. I'll take care of it.

(*GORDON moves to open the ice chest.*)

SALLY. Dad! Stop it, please!

(*CLAY POUND, 40, enters. HE is a farmer and stern in demeanor and appearance. HE is dressed in cowboy boots and wears a weathered Stetson hat.*)

CLAY. Good morning. (*CLAY casually walks over and flips off the TV.*)

GORDON. What are you doing?

CLAY. Coming to visit you ...

GORDON. You turned off my news.

CLAY. Not time for it yet.
GORDON. Almost.
CLAY. Can't think with that dern thing blasting.
GORDON. Say hello to your sister.
CLAY. Hi, Sally.

(SALLY goes to CLAY and gives him a hug—it is endured but not returned.)

SALLY. Clay ...
CLAY. I haven't seen you in two years. You look kinda beat up.
SALLY. Do I? Well, I feel fine.
GORDON. Did you know she was coming by here?
CLAY. I believe Jack mentioned it.
SALLY. It's good to see you, Clay.
CLAY. Dad, I want to borrow that pair of wire cutters I gave you last summer.
GORDON. What for?
CLAY. (*Sarcastically.*) I'm going to cut down all the electrical wires from the highway to your house.
GORDON. I don't understand why you would want to give me a gift if you needed it for yourself ... it doesn't make any sense.
CLAY. I gave the dern thing to you so's it'd be here when I needed it.
GORDON. I don't want you tearing through my tool shed looking.
CLAY. Maybe you'll find 'em for me so's I won't upset your private domain.

GORDON. To keep you out of it, I will. (*GORDON rises—begins to exit.*) The only one that don't make a mess out there's Maude.

CLAY. I understand that.

(*GORDON exits.*)

SALLY. Clay, I ...

CLAY. Shut up and listen, it won't take him a second to find those cutters.

SALLY. What?

CLAY. Mother could be in trouble. It was on the news this morning. There was a church group taken hostage over in Israel. Sounds like her bunch. I called that tourist office in Austin, the fellow in charge says he's been having trouble contacting anyone and he's getting worried. Sally, there's a real possibility she's been kidnapped.

SALLY. What are you saying?

CLAY. By Shiite highjackers.

SALLY. Jesus.

CLAY. I don't want Dad hearing about it until we know more for certain.

SALLY. But, you just said they had her ...

CLAY. No I didn't. I said they *might* have her. Nothing is certain right now, but I don't want the old man worrying himself sick.

SALLY. (*Panicking.*) What would we do without Mother?

CLAY. Stop it, now! You've got to keep Dad from finding out.

SALLY. Me?

CLAY. Yes.

SALLY. How?

CLAY. Keep him busy. Occupy him with something.

GORDON. (*Re-enters with the wire cutters.*) Hanging right where I left them. (*Hands the cutters to Clay.*) Don't let them kids of yours use 'em, they'll lose 'em for sure.

CLAY. I won't. So, I'll be seeing you.

GORDON. Off already?

CLAY. Got a big day ahead.

GORDON. Need any help?

CLAY. No. I've got a couple of deals at the Brahman Bull Sale.

GORDON. Are you selling or buying?

CLAY. Buying.

GORDON. I might go down there myself. You want to go with me, Sally?

SALLY. I really don't have time, Dad. Clay, I've got to head on out of here real soon.

GORDON. Lord, you just got here.

SALLY. I know, but I have an important date.

GORDON. I thought you was already married ...

SALLY. I am.

GORDON. Then what are you doing with a date?

SALLY. Dad ...

CLAY. Aw, Sally, you can stay here with Dad for the day or even longer if he wants you to ... he hasn't seen you in some time.

SALLY. I can?

CLAY. Sure. I'll drop back late this afternoon. We'll discuss that matter you needed my advice about then.

SALLY. Well, I guess I can stay until this afternoon.

CLAY. You two stay out of the sun. S'pose to be in the high 90's before it's over.

SALLY. Clay?

CLAY. I've got to go. The earlier you get to the auction, the more you can get accomplished.

GORDON. Well, you're already late by my clock.

(CLAY exits.)

SALLY. Clay! *(SALLY starts for the door.)*

GORDON. Let him go! I don't see why you'd need Clay's advice about one dern thing. You could ask my advice if you needed an opinion about something. *(GORDON turns on the TV.)* I don't remember you asking me a thing since you was knee-high but for money to squander at the picture show.

(SALLY quickly walks to the TV and turns it off.)

GORDON. Why'd you do that?

SALLY. You said you'd fix me some breakfast, didn't you?

GORDON. It's time for my news program.

SALLY. Dad, how about some good ole eggs and hominy grits.

GORDON. Lord, that would take some fixing and my news is coming here any second.

SALLY. I've got a hankering for grits, Dad! Please?

GORDON. *(Moves for the TV.)* Go on ... wreck the kitchen, Maude ain't here to see it. I'll clean her up after you've et.

(SALLY moves in front of him.)

GORDON. Get out from the television, Sally.

SALLY. Dad?

GORDON. Thunderation, what?

SALLY. I've got to tell you something.

GORDON. Well make it snappy.

SALLY. (*Tragically.*) Dad, my cat, Maurice, is dead.

GORDON. That's an important piece of news for me to know.

SALLY. He's in the ice chest.

GORDON. You said you had beer in that ice chest.

SALLY. (*Sobbing.*) Under the beer is my cat, Maurice.

GORDON. I don't believe you're sober.

SALLY. Of course I'm sober. (*Heartbroken.*) I've got Maurice's corpse on ice.

GORDON. You brought a cat dead from New York City?

SALLY. He was alive when I left.

GORDON. Why didn't you just toss him out on the side of the road?

SALLY. (*Incredulous.*) Dad ... Maurice was my best friend. (*Pause.*) He's traveled with me dozens of times but this trip I was half way through Tennessee when he just laid down in my lap and died. (*Reverently.*) He was sixteen last week. I want to bury him on the hill next to Old Red and Sappy.

GORDON. I'm glad I didn't open it up, it might have given me a heart attack.

SALLY. We've got to bury him, Dad.

GORDON. That'll wait until after my news.

(*GORDON turns on the TV. SALLY walks around and pulls the plug from the wall.*)

GORDON. Are you out of you mind? Plug that back in the wall.

SALLY. I've just told you about the death of my most favorite pet in my entire life and you can sit and listen to the news?

(GORDON takes the plug out of Sally's hand and plugs it into the wall. SALLY raises her voice over the television.)

SALLY. Because it was my pet, my friend ... I've kept it with me for sixteen years, through it all this cat was a pillar of strength.

(GORDON turns up the volume.
ANNOUNCER'S VOICE comes over the TV.)

ANNOUNCER. A crowded tourist bus was highjacked today by two Shiite Moslem highjackers outside of Jerusalem. Several American tourist groups were reported in the area, however, the identification of the group is not known at this time.

SALLY. Sweet Jesus!

(SALLY turns down the volume. GORDON is evidently upset. His BREATHING becomes irregular.)

SALLY. Dad?

GORDON. That's your Mother, as sure as I'm sitting here.

SALLY. (*Feigns a cavalier attitude toward the highjacking news.*) Those guys would be in deep shit if they started messing around with Maude Pound and Thelma Ferris.

GORDON. She's over there in Jerusalem.

SALLY. Dad, this isn't Mother's group.

GORDON. How would you know?

SALLY. I just know!

GORDON. I don't think you know a thing about it ... I'm going to call Clay. (*GORDON goes to the phone and dials.*) Hello? Clay? I think your Mother has been taken captive, I surely do. They just said it on the television. (*Pause.*) Well, you don't think so? (*GORDON hands the phone to SALLY and sits.*) The devil. He wants to talk to you.

SALLY. (*On the phone.*) Clay? No. Everything is under control. Heh, what do you take me for? Right. Goodbye. (*Pause.*) Dad, Clay says we've got to stay calm until we get more definite word. Dad?

GORDON. (*Rises up from his chair.*) I better pack my bag.

SALLY. What?

GORDON. I have to go get your Mother.

SALLY. Get Mother?

GORDON. That's what I said.

SALLY. No way.

GORDON. I ain't asking your permission.

SALLY. I have to stay here and you have to stay here with me!

GORDON. I'm going to dial that emergency number she gave me, find out where she is this exact moment. I'll call her and if she's not there, I'll have to go get her.

(*GORDON reaches Maude's desk. HE pulls a slip from a neat stack of papers.*) I can't do it, my hands are starting to shake. You dial this number for me.

SALLY. Take it easy, Dad.

GORDON. Do as I say! I'll read it off for you.

SALLY. Christ, alright.

GORDON. It's 214-555-2003.

SALLY. That's your number.

GORDON. (*Thrusts the paper at her.*) Well, find the right one. I don't have my reading glasses. (*GORDON stumbles.*)

SALLY. Sit down, Dad. You're breathing heavy. Come on, now. (*SALLY helps him in his armchair.*) You want me to get you a glass of water?

GORDON. That'd do.

(*SALLY goes to the kitchen sink and gets a glass of water.*)

GORDON. I'll never forgive her for going off alone. She should have gone to see the Grand Canyon like I told her. I was the one bought the vacation, I should have been allowed to choose where we was going. Them people are fanatics. They ain't going to care if you're with the Methodist, the Baptist, they don't even care if you're Catholic or a Jew, they just care about blowing up anybody who ain't believing like they do. If I ever get her back home I'm going to have it put in my will that she doesn't get any of my money until she signs an agreement not to travel outside the United States.

(*SALLY brings him a glass of water.*

GORDON gulps it down.)

SALLY. Dad, this is a big mix up.

GORDON. I'll probably die going to get her. But, it's no matter, I'll sit here for a few minutes to catch my breath, then I'll be leaving.

SALLY. Dad, look, I've got to bury my cat. Now, let's just go at things systematically. Help me bury Maurice before it gets too hot, then we can call the emergency number for the travel agency, find out where Mother is scheduled to be today. And, now, Dad ... we've got to wait for Clay ...

GORDON. The devil! I'm headed for Jerusalem.

SALLY. You can't just rush into a foreign country. Do you have a passport?

GORDON. If you won't take me, I'll catch me a bus on the highway that would get me as far as Texarkana.

SALLY. No, no, no need for that ... we've got a car, we've got *my* car. But I'm not leaving Maurice in that ice chest one second longer.

GORDON. The devil with that cat.

SALLY. *(Taking control.)* Now, Dad ... just settle down. Where's a shovel?

GORDON. Out by the barn, if Clay's kids ain't lost it.

SALLY. C'mon, Dad. Help me find the shovel. I need you. I hate funerals.

GORDON. You ought to throw that cat out with the garbage.

SALLY. Is that what you want us to do with you when you pass to the other side?

GORDON. Be fine by me. Let's make this snappy. I've not got time for no drawn-out affair.

(The LIGHTS go to BLACK as THEY exit to the outside.
High noon. As the LIGHTS come up, GORDON and
SALLY sit at the kitchen table. SALLY is drinking
beer. THEY are playing dominoes. GORDON lays
down his winning domino.)

GORDON. That beats you five times in a row.

SALLY. You're keeping score?

GORDON. *(Checking his pocket watch.)* That travel
agency fellow said he would call me back in one hour. It's
been one hour and ten minutes.

SALLY. He said he'd call when he had any new word.

GORDON. He said he'd call me here.

SALLY. Yes, and he will. He'll have all the
information, where Maude Pound will be every second in
the hour.

GORDON. You can say what you want to, but I
believe that office is trying to cover up Maude's
whereabouts. I find it hard to believe that not one person in
the dern place knows a thing about that group.

SALLY. Aren't you enjoying beating the stuffings out
of me?

GORDON. Ain't no fun if you're a better player than
your competition. Maude beats me ten games to one.
(Pause.) Only time I can remember you ever playing that
piano Maude bought you was when you was trying to get
out of washing the dishes.

SALLY. Ridiculous.

GORDON. I don't think you would have ever made a
performer like Jack did. He could play any tune on any
instrument you could name and never make a

mistake.(*Pause.*) I never heard you play one song that you didn't make a mistake and have to stop and start out again. (*Pause.*) Now Jack tells me, you want to be a serious writer. I'd like to know. What good are serious stories? If you want to read a serious story, read the Bible.

SALLY. I believe he was referring to being a serious writer as in, making a living.

GORDON. Well ...

(Pause.)

SALLY. Apparently Jack didn't tell you about my novel ...

GORDON. (*Interested.*) You wrote a book?

SALLY. About you ...

GORDON. The devil!

SALLY. Tracing my ancestral history from the arrival of the first hardened convicts deported to the State of Georgia by King George down to Gordon Pound's tiny but powerful kingdom in East Texas.

GORDON. You wrote a story about that?

SALLY. Don't worry. The names were changed.

GORDON. Wouldn't have to change my name. I ain't never done a thing I'd be ashamed of anyone knowing about ... I'm an honest man.

SALLY. Pleasure to know you.

GORDON. Not that you couldn't write a story about the Pound family. I believe they are more interesting than most.

SALLY. My sentiments precisely ...

(Pause.)

GORDON. It is a mystery to me how you could lay down a shovel without marking the spot and expect to find it in two hundred acres of pasture. It's under the leaves.

SALLY. I'll find the blankety blank shovel.

GORDON. Clay is going to be mad at you. That was his favorite shovel.

SALLY. I'll buy a new one.

GORDON. I'd rather he was mad at you than at me. Maude thinks that boy hung the moon but that's just because they like to get together and work themselves silly. (*Pause.*) I'll have to find me some woman who likes to sit and play dominoes when it gets this hot. I could have my pick over at the old folks' home.

SALLY. None as good looking as my mother.

GORDON. They's a couple ain't half bad. (*Pause.*) I can't see why a fellow would waste his hard earned money on beer. It ain't got no kick to it. Not like liquor. Maude never tasted whiskey her entire life. Don't care for the smell of it. I never took a drink until I was twelve or more years old. I wouldn't have taken one then but your Uncle Dot forced one down my throat. Said I wasn't a man if I couldn't down a swallow of moonshine and he wouldn't have people talking about any brother of his being a sissy.

SALLY. It's a wonder you didn't turn gay.

GORDON. What's that you say?

SALLY. Homosexuality is related to childhood trauma.

GORDON. I heard that on the television. Dr. Ruth says it happens before they's six years old. Them fellows get a hankering for the other end of the cow at a real early age.

SALLY. The other end?

GORDON. The dickens! You know what I'm saying. (*GORDON changes the subject quickly.*) Jack says you work for some magazine.

SALLY. I've been a writer for *Newsweek* for quite a few years now.

(*Pause.*)

GORDON. You're awful quiet.

SALLY. I'm thinking.

GORDON. Well, say something. You sitting there makes me nervous.

SALLY. What would you like to hear?

GORDON. Express an opinion or something.

SALLY. I think I'll go to Rio de Janeiro my next vacation ...

GORDON. Are you absolutely certain you gave that agent fellow the right number to call?

SALLY. For the hundreth time, yes.

GORDON. I've always believed one of your problems is lack of money. If you didn't stop changing professions every ten minutes you'd have more security.

SALLY. I'm telling you, right now, I have a top level position in a national magazine. I have published several award winning short stories, I have a play running in an Off-Broadway theatre, and currently I'm publishing an epic novel based loosely on your life. Needless to say, the combined monies from all these projects has set me up for life.

GORDON. You don't dress like you make a living. (*Pause.*) Well, tell me if I'm wrong.

SALLY. It's summertime, Dad. Otherwise, I would have worn one of my several mink coats for the drive home.

GORDON. Anyone who would spend hard earned money on a mink coat is a fool.

SALLY. (*Losing her temper.*) Well, since I paid for my entire education, Dad. And, since you were too cheap to lay out two cents on me or what I was interested in, you have no right to tell me what to do. I believe that categorically proves I'm no fool.

GORDON. (*Lays down his final domino with much relish.*) There. I'm out again. Let's see. How many points do I get?

SALLY. Twenty-five.

GORDON. Twenty-five? That's mighty little. Did you cheat me?

SALLY. Why would I want to cheat at dominoes? (*Pause.*) I wonder what the hell has happened to Clay ...

GORDON. Clay don't give a dern about nobody.

SALLY. I thought he'd be here by now ...

GORDON. He ought to be helping me get to Israel.

SALLY. (*Gets up, stretches, looks out at the thermometer.*) It's 92 degrees out there.

GORDON. Go out to the mailbox. See if anything came in ...

SALLY. Dad ... I checked it twice this morning.

GORDON. Well, check it again.

SALLY. It's too dern hot!

GORDON. I'll go.

SALLY. No, now, there's nothing out there.

GORDON. They might send a telegram.

SALLY. If we got a telegram, they'd drive it right up to the front door.

GORDON. Maude is too busy flirting with that preacher to write me a letter.

SALLY. I wouldn't blame her. As I remember, he's a good looking guy.

GORDON. Always searching for a handout. I never asked a thing from any man in my whole life, now there's people living off my wages that never did a single lick of work in their lives.

SALLY. I'm sure they're grateful.

GORDON. Haven't received a single thank you. (*Pause.*) You think if she got herself killed over there, they'd send the body back?

SALLY. Dad, please, be serious.

GORDON. Those Shittites shoot those people if they step out of line. If anything happens to her before I get there, it would be justice for her leaving me alone.

SALLY. That's a rotten thing to say.

GORDON. She said she'd stand behind the preacher if there was any trouble. I think he'd be the first one they'd shoot. Stopping a bullet is about all he's good for.

SALLY. You seem to be disenchanted with almost everyone.

GORDON. I never did like anybody but Maude. But, she don't care about me or she would not have taken this trip. (*Pause.*) I never did have much to say to women.

SALLY. I never heard a lot from men that was worth listening to.

GORDON. Better not let that husband of yours hear you talking like that. (*Pause.*) I was right surprised when Maude told me you were getting married.

SALLY. Why was that?

GORDON. I didn't think you'd find one that would agree to marry you at your age.

SALLY. Dad ...

GORDON. If my memory serves me correct, you'd be thirty-six years at 7:00 tonight. It's hard for woman to find a man at that age. That's what all the television talk shows say.

SALLY. I'll be thirty-five. And I've had more than my share of men in my life.

GORDON. Let me ask you this, how does the world appear to you at thirty-six?

SALLY. It's *thirty-five* and I don't know.

(The PHONE rings. GORDON answers it quickly.)

GORDON. Hello! Who? Don. Thunder. We ain't got time to talk to you, now. She's here. Just a second. (*GORDON hands the phone to SALLY.*) It's your husband. Keep it short.

SALLY. (*Takes the phone. Lovingly.*) Hello. Darling! I can't talk now. Goodbye. (*SALLY hangs up the phone.*) That short enough?

GORDON. That was the only time you've done what I asked you to without an argument. (*Pause.*) You might have made him mad.

SALLY. Most understanding man in the world ... (*SALLY begins to search through her knapsack.*)

GORDON. I believe that agency man was lying to you about calling me back.

SALLY. If he said he would call, he'll call.

GORDON. How do you know, you don't even know the man.

SALLY. Leave it alone, Dad!

GORDON. I ought to be leaving right this minute. Of course, Maude will be sorry to see me arrive. It'll spoil her good time with the preacher.

SALLY. (*Throws her knapsack down in despair.*) What are you talking about?

GORDON. She's having an affair with the preacher, lying in the same bed, this very minute.

SALLY. Oh?

GORDON. That's why she was so tickled when I couldn't go.

SALLY. There is a rather obvious age difference. The preacher that I remember, black hair, blue eyes, around six feet ... that's the one, right?

GORDON. Right.

SALLY. He can't possibly be over thirty-five—forty at the most.

GORDON. Young whippersnapper.

SALLY. Mother is seventy-six years old.

GORDON. And four months.

SALLY. That's my point.

GORDON. That's the fashion nowadays.

SALLY. Younger men with old women?

GORDON. That's right.

SALLY. What about the other minor detail?

GORDON. What's that?

SALLY. The preacher has a wife.

GORDON. His wife is sleeping with the Baptist preacher so she don't care what he does.

SALLY. I don't believe it.

GORDON. You don't have to believe it for it to be true.

SALLY. I know for an absolute fact that Maude Pound has always been faithful to you.

GORDON. You don't know.

SALLY. Yes, I do.

GORDON. How?

SALLY. She told me.

GORDON. Told you?

SALLY. She told me she has never been in bed or made love or had sex with any man but you.

GORDON. When did she tell you that?

SALLY. Last year.

GORDON. That might have been the case last year but I believe she's taken up with the preacher since then. (*GORDON exits.*)

SALLY. Where are you going? (*No answer.*) What the hell is going on?

(GORDON enters with his suitcase.)

SALLY. Ok, Dad. This has gone far enough. Put your suitcase back in your room and let's play some more dominoes!

GORDON. It may not appear to you as such, but I am still the captain of my fate.

SALLY. You agreed that we'd wait for the phone call.

(GORDON picks up his suitcase and heads for the door. SALLY grabs it from him and sits down on it.)

SALLY. We're not going anywhere. Mother is at the wailing wall today. All right?

GORDON. I have to borrow your car. Maude's ain't running.

SALLY. No way.

GORDON. I've got your keys.

SALLY. Where did you get my keys?

GORDON. I ain't going to fight you for that suitcase. I don't need no more than the clothes I got on my back. So long, been good to know you.

(GORDON heads for the door. SALLY stands in front of him.)

GORDON. Get out of my way.

SALLY. No way. You're not taking my car, Dad. We've got to stay here!

GORDON. I'll go out the kitchen door.

(SALLY quickly intercepts GORDON in front of the kitchen door.)

SALLY. Hand over the car keys, Dad.

GORDON. I'll just drive my tractor to town if I don't take your car.

SALLY. Then drive the damn tractor.

GORDON. I can't, it's busted since the winter.

SALLY. (*Raging.*) Cough up the keys!

GORDON. I ain't.

SALLY. You will!

GORDON. You ain't telling me what to do in my own house.

SALLY. I am telling you what to do if I have to fight you with my fists. You aren't going anywhere.

GORDON. Then fight me.

(SALLY flies into a rage. SHE lightly tackles him to the ground and the FATHER and DAUGHTER fight, haphazardly. No hard knocks, but emotionally draining. It is mostly rolling around. GORDON is beaten.)

GORDON. Hold on. I quit. Land sakes alive!

SALLY. Are you all right? (*Pause.*) Let me help you up.

(SALLY helps GORDON to the couch.)

GORDON. Let me sit a minute. You're stronger than you look.

(GORDON sits. SALLY becomes irrationally angry.)

SALLY. Have you totally lost it? Logic, logic would tell you that you haven't a prayer of a chance to find Mother. It's not even funny. God, you piss me off! If you'd just listen to somebody! Hell, you never listened to me as a kid, you never listened to me as an adult. Never enough.

GORDON. Get out of my house.

SALLY. No.

GORDON. Then I will.

SALLY. You wouldn't make it one mile.

GORDON. I'll never forgive you for this.

SALLY. Get in line. Get in the fucking line of men who aren't going to forgive me. I'm always trying to get some fucking man to like me, I was always trying to get my father and brothers to like me but I don't care anymore if you like me or not. You know? I don't give a good goddamn. Because I can beat you up. I certainly can.

GORDON. I want Maude.

SALLY. I can't help that ...

GORDON. You wait until Clay gets here.

SALLY. You always delighted in scaring the shit out of me. Well, no more, no sir, no way!

GORDON. You have lost all control.

SALLY. Oh, no. I'm gaining control. I'm not going to let you or anybody else tell me I'm stupid, or foolish, or insensitive, or a boor, or a whore, or whatever you'd like for me to be to appease your guilty conscience.

(GORDON pulls himself up from the chair.)

SALLY. I'm taking all the keys to everything with wheels and hiding them in case you feel like sneaking off.

GORDON. I'm going to my room.

SALLY. That's a good idea.

(GORDON POUND exits. SALLY sits and stares at the pair of car keys. SHE throws them on the kitchen table.)

SALLY. Christ.

(The front door opens. CLAY POUND enters. HE whispers.)

CLAY. Sally?

SALLY. Clay? Finally!

CLAY. Where's Dad?

SALLY. He's in his room. Thank God, you're here! He has gone absolutely berserk!

CLAY. Pipe down. Any news?

SALLY. No, but Clay ... we had a fight.

CLAY. I don't know why you let him listen to the news.

SALLY. A knock-down drag out fight.

CLAY. (*Teasing.*) Why, Sally, you ought to be ashamed of yourself—beating the shit out of an old man.

SALLY. (*Desperate.*) I've got to get out of here, Clay. I can't stay any longer. He's mopping the floor with what's left of my sanity. Did you bring the money?

CLAY. I've got two deals pending at the sale. I've got to get right back. You'll just have to cool your butt 'til we get this mess straight.

SALLY. Clay, please, just let me borrow the money and get out of here ... I'm in a lot of trouble.

CLAY. Don't start shoveling horse shit, Sally.

SALLY. I've got to be in Austin by midnight!

CLAY. Calm down.

SALLY. No!

CLAY. You want me to tell him what's going on with you?

SALLY. No.

CLAY. Then pipe down.

SALLY. (*Quietly urgent.*) Look! I'm in a very serious jam here. I came home because Jack promised I could borrow the money from him then I find out I have to borrow it from you but no matter who I borrow the money from, I've *got* to get it and pay these people by midnight tonight because if I don't pay these people, they're going to come looking for me.

CLAY. Sorry, little sister, give them a call—tell them you'll be late.

SALLY. I can't do that ...

CLAY. If you want the money to give them, you'll do it.

SALLY. Wait a damn minute! You promised me.

CLAY. I don't give a fuck about promises right now ...

SALLY. Clay, I know this ... if somebody hadn't promised me ... I'd be out of the country ...

CLAY. What about your mother, Sally? Don't you care what's happened to her?

SALLY. Jesus. Of course I care, Clay. But I can't help her. She's over there and there's nothing we can do.

CLAY. Look, I'll be back before sundown. That's still time for you to get to Austin.

SALLY. Clay, please give me the money now ... I'll go to Austin, take care of my business and be back before morning.

CLAY. I can't risk leaving the old man alone. (*Pause.*) What if we find out Mother's dead?

SALLY. Clay, don't say that ... (*SALLY begins to cry.*)

CLAY. Don't get so upset, nothing's certain.

SALLY. Then don't say things like that.

CLAY. Look, little sister, I don't have a lot of cash just lying around ... that's what I'm working on.

SALLY. Why can't your wife stay with Dad?

CLAY. Connie's got two of the kids home with the chicken pox.

SALLY. Then one of the other kids? One that's not sick?

CLAY. Sally, if you want to borrow three thousand dollars from me, I have to go back to the sale to get it. You're going to have to stay with the old man until I can get back ... I'll be back as soon as I can. I suggest you call these people and tell them you may be late. *(CLAY exits.)*

SALLY. Goodbye, Clay. (*SALLY sits on the couch—stunned. SHE takes a pill. A beat. SHE goes to the phone, dials.*) Hello? Ramon? This is Sally Pound. Glad I could catch you ...Where am I? Somewhere in East Texas ... ha ha. I might be a little bit late tonight because of this family problem. My mother has been kidnapped. No. Seriously. That's where I am ... at my parent's ... Ramon ... *(Pause.)* I'm not trying to hide. It's serious here. *(Pause.)* I have the money. C'mon ... I'm spelling it out for you, I *have* the money. It's right here in my pocket ... Ramon? Look, you're not going to like this, but I have to stay with my father until they locate my ... Ramon ... don't be like that ... you told me you were a fair man. *(Pause.)* Yes ... I understand. (*Ramon hangs up on the other end. SALLY is left with a dial tone. SHE stares into the receiver.*) Doesn't anybody say goodbye anymore?

END OF ACT I

ACT II

SALLY sits on the couch looking through photographs,
high school yearbooks, etc. GORDON enters and stares
intently at her. HE goes to the window, looks out at his
land.

GORDON. If you don't help me do something, I don't
know what ... to find out about that little gal of mine, I
may as well walk off into the Covington bottoms.

SALLY. Couldn't sleep?

GORDON. Hell, no. Can't sleep, can't eat, can't walk,
can't do nothing. I sit up half the night. After fifty-two
years of sleeping in the same bed, Maude won't sleep with
me no more. She says I wrop myself up in the blanket and
she near sweats herself sick. Well, I get cold. (*Pause.*)
Maude sits staring out that kitchen window, she says she's
waiting for that big crane that lives on the pool to fly off,
but I know she's waiting for me to go on and die so she
can fly off. She sees them other widow women getting
around without any trouble.

SALLY. C'mon now, Dad.

GORDON. My body is giving way. I'm a hindrance to
everybody. I can't keep cows anymore because I can't walk
my own fence row. The only thing I could plant would be
turnips because you just broadcast the seeds but I couldn't
bend down to pick them once they was growed.

SALLY. That's not true.

GORDON. The devil it's not. You just don't know. You're never around here. Day before yesterday, I went out to saddle up Peanuts and take her for a ride on her birthday. She was twenty-one—near as old as me. That dagblasted pony stepped on my foot while I was saddling her up and I let out a good yell. She spooked and sided me up against the barn and I was trapped, by God. Couldn't move. I shoved and pushed and knocked and beat on that horse for ten minutes, but I didn't have the strength to get out from her. Clay rescued me after a spell. My foot had swelled up so bad, had to cut my boot off. (*Pause.*) Not two hours later, Peanuts dropped dead in the pasture. I believe that pony died of shame for not having the sense to move off my foot.

(*GORDON starts to exit. SALLY rises up and watches him go.*)

SALLY. Dad?

(*HE stops.*)

SALLY. I'm sorry you lost your horse. I know how you must feel.
GORDON. You're not going to equate my losing Peanuts with you losing that dern cat of yours, are you?
SALLY. Well, yes, I am.
GORDON. Peanuts was worth a dern site more than any cat. That mare was the best cutting horse in East Texas.
SALLY. Peanuts hadn't cut in a while, Dad.

GORDON. She earned *her* rest. That cat of yours never did a thing but eat and sleep. I don't place the two in the same category.

SALLY. Forget it.

GORDON. I will. And I wish, more than anything I know, that you would help me find Maude.

SALLY. There's nothing we can do but wait, Dad.

GORDON. I'm so dern mad at you I could spit. (*GORDON goes to the phone. Dials a number.*)

SALLY. Who are you calling?

GORDON. None of your business ... (*Pause.*) Sheriff Rubens? This is Gordon Pound. Have you got any news on your Teletype there about those hostages over in Israel? Well, you know Maude is over there in Jerusalem. Yep. Well, I called those travel people in Austin and the fellow said he'd call me back with her location but he hasn't. (*Pause.*) No, that's what I'm telling you ... he hasn't. I'm beginning to break out with hives for lack of word. (*Pause.*) Well, that's easy for you to say but your wife ain't the one that's over there. I want you to do me a favor. I ain't got a car since my accident and this heat will make a feller faint to walk in it. I want you or one of your boys, there, to come over here and drive me to town so I can catch me a bus. (*Pause.*) I ain't calling Clay, I'm calling you ... well, dern your hide. (*GORDON hangs up the phone and dials again.*) Connie? Is Clay there? He isn't? Come over here and get me. What? Yeah, she's here. Stay put? I don't aim to stay put ... well, dern your hide. (*GORDON hangs up the phone.*)

SALLY. No luck?

GORDON. That wife of Clay's ain't got a civil word in her vocabulary. And I'll not vote for that sheriff a second time. (*GORDON turns on the television. Soap operas can be heard. HE switches stations ... more soap operas ... HE switches again ... more soap operas. HE turns down the volume and sits in front of the television waiting.*)

SALLY. Dad? You're going to make yourself sick if you keep this up.

GORDON. I want you to swear to keep secret anything we might say to one another from here on out. My patience is at an end and I won't be held accountable.

SALLY. I swear.

GORDON. On the Holy Bible?

SALLY. (*Ironically.*) Lend me three thousand dollars and I'll swear on anything.

GORDON. I thought you was rich.

SALLY. A person can't have too much money.

GORDON. (*Gets up and starts moving around the room, irrationally.*) Either you let me borrow your car or take me yourself to find out about Maude, or I'm going to do something drastic.

SALLY. I'm not going to offer the use of my car to a crazy person.

GORDON. Then you'll be an accomplice.

SALLY. Accomplice to what, Dad?

GORDON. (*Ominously.*) I ain't saying.

SALLY. If anything happens to you while I'm here, Clay will hold me directly responsible.

GORDON. Maude's lost and ain't never coming back. I might as well shoot myself in the head.

SALLY. Dad, threatening suicide ain't going to get it.

GORDON. I'll shoot myself. I swear I will.

SALLY. Dad!

GORDON. It's not being dead that worries me, it's the transition. (*Pause.*) You don't get your insurance money if it's a suicide, and if Maude ain't dead already, she's going to need every cent she can get when I'm gone to find her another husband.

SALLY. I expect she'll give every cent she has to the preacher the minute you're in the coffin.

GORDON. You may not think you're talking serious, now, but I believe what you're saying to be the God's truth.

SALLY. Aw, Dad. (*SALLY sits up on the couch and looks at her father sympathetically. There is a long pause.*) Is there any sane, logical thing I can do that will make you feel better?

GORDON. Start your car and take me to get Maude.

(SALLY goes to her knapsack and searches.)

GORDON. That's the tenth time I've seen you search through that bag. What in the devil are you looking for?

SALLY. My medication.

GORDON. What sort of medication?

SALLY. I have hypoglycemia menstrual cramps resulting from ...

GORDON. Hold it there. You don't have to go any further. I don't need to know everything.

SALLY. All right. (*After a pause, SALLY pulls a bottle of Jack Daniels out of her knapsack.*)

GORDON. That won't help you, but it might help me.

SALLY. Really? Well ... O.K. Let's have a couple of drinks, and ... here's my offer, Dad, we'll drive to Austin and talk to that agency man personally ... then ...

GORDON. Are you pulling my leg?

SALLY. Hell, no. I'm serious.

GORDON. You promise me?

SALLY. I promise. I don't want to be party to any suicide attempts. If that man in Austin hasn't called us back in one hour, we'll leave. And if he does call and he thinks there's a possibility that Mother is in a jam, we'll have him book the two of us straight to Jerusalem. This will take money.

GORDON. I've got three dollars. You didn't bring any money with you?

SALLY. Not safe to travel with cash.

GORDON. Well, we'll stop at the bank.

SALLY. How much money have you got in the bank?

GORDON. Depends.

SALLY. On what ...

GORDON. What I'm using it for.

SALLY. To go find Maude Pound, your wife.

GORDON. I have enough to do that.

SALLY. Perhaps we could arrange something ... (*SALLY gets two glasses and pours them a drink.*) I never saw you take a drink in my life.

GORDON. I'm dern upset ... Don't you go telling Maude you saw me take a drink.

SALLY. Strictly entre nous.

GORDON. Let's just keep it between us.

SALLY. That's what I said.

GORDON. You did?

SALLY. Yep, but I said it in French.

GORDON. Dern. This is America, speak English.

SALLY. It's probably a new experience for you ... drinking liquor out of a glass instead of a quart jar.

GORDON. Could be.

SALLY. Things are looking up.

GORDON. Don't see how a container would make a difference.

SALLY. Trust me. I suppose ice cubes would be out of the question ...

GORDON. If the Lord wanted liquor to have ice cubes in it, he'd a made it taste the same as ice tea.

(Pause.)

SALLY. Let's get drunk and go find a party in Austin.

GORDON. Wouldn't want you to get too drunk to drive. *(Pause.)* Dern her hide for making me worry like this!

SALLY. My mother is the best woman you'll ever find.

(Pause.)

GORDON. I think I can hold my liquor a sight better than you.

SALLY. That remains to be seen.

(GORDON takes the drink, sips it and then downs the entire glass of liquor in one long swallow.)

SALLY. So much for sipping whiskey. *(SALLY tosses her drink down. Coughs.)*

GORDON. You can't drink. *(GORDON refills his glass.)* If anything has happened to Maude, I suppose I'll live here by myself until I die. Without her, it won't be long. I'll die of loneliness and that will be fine. But, no matter what, don't put me in that old folks' home they got in town. That's a death house. When a feller checks into that place he don't check out.

SALLY. I wouldn't have anything to say about it.

GORDON. I'd like to know why not?

SALLY. Clay makes that type of decision.

GORDON. The dickens he does. You got to stand up for me.

SALLY. Why?

GORDON. Because I'm telling you to do it.

SALLY. When did you ever stand up for me?

GORDON. They's been lots of times.

SALLY. That's bullshit. My mother is my only ally in this family. You never said two words to me until I was fifteen and wrecked the Chevy.

GORDON. What if I was sick and couldn't speak for myself?

SALLY. You're not sick.

GORDON. I might get sick.

SALLY. Well, anyhow, it wouldn't come to that.

GORDON. How do you know?

SALLY. I have a picture of you dying in some adventurous setting.

GORDON. I always saw it that way but sometimes it don't work out like you plan. What would become of me without Maude? *You* would be the only woman in my life.

SALLY. Nothing is going to happen to Mother.

GORDON. And I would have to come live with you.

SALLY. My life style is a little unorthodox, Dad.

GORDON. You'd just have to change the way you do things.

SALLY. Well, we'll cross that creek when we come to it.

GORDON. (*Pours himself another drink.*) You probably don't realize that I'm an alcoholic.

SALLY. You are?

GORDON. I can control it when Maude's around because she'd skin me alive if she thought I was drinking. (*GORDON downs the second glass.*) If I hadn't have met Maude, I would have turned out a skid row bum.

SALLY. That's incredible. I had no idea.

GORDON. Now, you ... you've done nothing but drink since you been here.

SALLY. I'm in a lot of physical pain.

GORDON. Your oldest brother, Jack, he's an alcoholic...

SALLY. That, I know.

GORDON. He inherited it from me.

SALLY. Now I see.

GORDON. He can't take a drink of whiskey less he drinks enough to make him pass clean out. (*Pause.*) You could write you a story about this ... Seems to me, the biggest problem nowadays, is nobody is content with what they've got. They're always aiming toward something better, something more than what they have. Don't seem they take the time to enjoy what they already got. I was a simple man, proud to be a simple man. I enjoyed counting my cows, planting a garden, building a fence row and playing dominoes with Maude. I enjoyed square dancing with her more than anything I know. My arthritis got so bad I couldn't move fast. Then my mind started slipping and I got confused about which direction I was to go. We had to stop going after that but she never had one complaint about it.

SALLY. Things can get complicated.

GORDON. I'm right sorry I let Clay talk me into selling all my cows. (*Pause.*) Did you call your husband back?

SALLY. Later.

GORDON. You're happy with him?

SALLY. Delirious.

GORDON. I'm surprised.

SALLY. Well ...

GORDON. (*Lifts his glass.*) Cheers.

SALLY. Cheers.

(THEY drink.)

GORDON. I believe the person one chooses to marry says an awful lot about them.

SALLY. Yep.

GORDON. If I were you, I'd be careful of getting hooked up on dern pills, I don't care what kind they are. It doesn't matter what's wrong, doctors will prescribe something for you. They got me so dependent on different medication, I dern near have to take pills to stay mobile. I got to paste a pill next to my heart every single night of my life. My chest is sore as hell from pulling the dern things off. Then, I have to take this one to settle my stomach, that one to keep my blood circulating and lots of them that I'm not sure what they accomplish. (*Pause.*) Fifty years ago I would have been dead of natural causes by now. And, I think all these pills I take just depress the hell out of me. They make you think differently than you ought to be thinking. (*Pause*.) I 'most died of snakebite when I was ten years or so. It was before my mother died. There had come a big rainstorm and I was playing in back of our house where I came upon this rather odd looking hole in the ground. Looked down in it with one eye and a dern water moccasin jumped up out of that hole and bit me on the nose. (*Pause*.) Dad hitched up the mules to the wagon and took me to the doctor's. I was rightly glad it happened because my mother held me in her lap the entire six miles. That's all I remember of her.

SALLY. Well, she would have missed you if you had died.

GORDON. Not for long. She died of consumption not six months after.

SALLY. Jesus, Dad, that's awful.

GORDON. Oh, I've had a terrible life. When Maude and I are gone, you'll be getting a third of this farm.

SALLY. Me?

GORDON. You.

SALLY. I didn't know that.

GORDON. But you'd have to live in the same county as Clay if you was to keep it.

SALLY. Can't I keep it and live somewhere else?

*(GORDON pours himself a healthy portion. HE downs it.
   SALLY pours herself another and downs it.)*

GORDON. I'll tell you the truth, I never had any use for that husband of yours. There ain't nobody here but you and me, you can tell me the truth and ...

SALLY. Nothing to tell.

GORDON. I must say, I'm surprised he turned out as good as you say he did.

SALLY. I have a pretty good eye, Dad.

GORDON. There was a string of 'em where you must of been drunk.

SALLY. No problems this time.

GORDON. Maude will be glad to hear that. She worries that you're happy.

SALLY. She does?

GORDON. So do I. You may not believe it's so, but I think about you quite often.

(SALLY is silent as GORDON pours himself another drink. Both are getting drunk.)

GORDON. I believe we're getting along better, now. *(Pause.)* A month ago, I saw a sign at the drugstore about whale blubber pills. They was advertised to help you overcome heart attacks or cancer of the stomach. The Eskimos in Alaska take it. Makes them healthy their entire lives. Have you ever heard of an Eskimo being sick?

SALLY. Never.

GORDON. They get a lot of whale blubber in their diet. I bought some and started taking them but they upset my stomach. I told Clay about that and he stared at me like I didn't have a brain one. Called me a dern fool in front of Maude. He didn't have to talk to me like that. *(Pause.)* He would have thought I was pretty smart if those pills had worked. But, they didn't.

SALLY. *(Goes to the phonograph, looking through the record collection.)* All this talk about heart attacks and stomach cancer is depressing.

GORDON. I'd leave Maude's Victrola alone, now. She'll fuss if you scratch her records.

(SALLY selects a record, removes it from the cover and places it on the phonograph.)

GORDON. You said we were leaving for Austin right about now.

SALLY. I said one hour. We've got thirty nine minutes left.

(The MUSIC begins: a spirited Texas two-step.)

GORDON. I'll have to put that record back before we leave.

SALLY. I remember you and Mother dancing. You two always looked great on the dance floor.

GORDON. I never cared that much for it.

SALLY. Really?

GORDON. Never cared for it much at all.

SALLY. You love to dance. It's all right. You can admit it.

GORDON. I ain't admitting to nothing.

SALLY. *(Mischievously.)* What about it? You want to cut a rug?

GORDON. We ain't got the time for it.

SALLY. *(Doing a few dance steps, turning up the volume.)* Sure we have. Now, c'mon, Dad ... you used to dance me around on your feet.

GORDON. That was when you was still little.

SALLY. And I've improved a hellavu lot since then.

GORDON. (*Begrudgingly*.) Well, I ain't got on my dancing boots, but I'll give her a whirl ...

(THEY dance.
GORDON, perking up, does a great two-step.)

GORDON. Stop trying to lead.
SALLY. I'm not.
GORDON. The man's the one that leads.

(After a moment.)

SALLY. Am I doing better?
GORDON. You dance almost as good as Maude.
SALLY. Well, hell, I should. She's the one who taught me how.
GORDON. Here comes a dip. (*GORDON performs a rather daring dip.*)
SALLY. Yahoo.

(The front door opens and CLAY enters. The dancers are unaware of him until HE moves to pick up the bottle of Jack Daniels. THEY nod "hello's.")

CLAY. Having a party?
GORDON. Sure are ... come join us ...
SALLY. Clay!

(GORDON starts parading around the room, making up a dance. SALLY follows.)

GORDON. I'm as drunk as a skunk.

SALLY. I'm lit up as a hoot owl.

GORDON. I'm roasted as a rooster in love.

SALLY. I'm tanked as a tiger.

GORDON. I'm silly as a petunia.

SALLY. That's silly.

(THEY get the giggles.)

SALLY. Act natural. Now. Settle down.

GORDON. You'd best tell your face.

SALLY. All right.

(CLAY turns the MUSIC off.)

GORDON. Dern, Clay, we were just getting warmed up.

CLAY. I take it you're feeling better, Dad?

GORDON. Yeah. I took a turn for the better, that's what happened. There's Sally. She came all the way from New York by herself just to see me.

CLAY. That was good of her.

GORDON. It was. I was surprised. *(GORDON is suddenly uncomfortable in front of his serious son.)* Doggie! I'm a little tired all of a sudden. *(GORDON takes about five steps across the room and falls flat down on his butt. HE is so drunk he can't move.)*

CLAY. What the hell is going on here?

SALLY. *(Puzzled.)* Dad? Are you alright?

GORDON. Help me up.

(SALLY and CLAY help him to his feet. SALLY and GORDON are giggling.)

SALLY. It must have been your breakfast.

GORDON. Must of been. Something I et. My feet went right out from under me. That must have been a fairly funny sight.

CLAY. Both of you smell like breweries. He shouldn't be drinking. He's taking a lot of different medicine.

GORDON. It don't bother me.

CLAY. It's stupid, Dad.

GORDON. I'm just not too bright. Right, Sally?

CLAY. Between the two of you, there's not enough brains to hoe a garden.

SALLY. Come on now, Clay. We've had extenuating circumstances.

CLAY. You are something else. I have to practically bribe you to get you to stay here and then you feed him booze. Are you out of your mind?

GORDON. Who did you bribe? You had to bribe Sally?

SALLY. Clay, don't do this ...

CLAY. She'd have been outta here this morning if she didn't need money, she's in trouble and wants me to bail her out.

SALLY. It's worse than it sounds, Dad.

GORDON. Well, nobody has to take care of me, I take care of myself.

CLAY. Sure! Like day before yesterday, you almost got yourself trampled by your own horse?

SALLY. That's enough, Clay.

CLAY. The only way Mother would leave you was if Jack and I were close by to check on you ... because lately you can't seem to walk across the road alone without getting killed. Well, you ornery jackass, you treated Jack so bad he couldn't stay around you anymore. And I have a farm to run, I haven't got the time ... Mother's lost so now you're going to have to look out for yourself, you dern fool. She's in terrible danger and what are you doing ... getting drunk. I wanted her to go on this trip just so she could get away from you for an hour, for a day ...

SALLY. Clay, stop it!

CLAY. You drive everybody away from you!

(GORDON is "crushed." CLAY turns on Sally.)

CLAY. And you, what were you trying to do, kill him?

SALLY. We won't drink anymore, all right?

CLAY. I'm tired of your selfishness. Nobody has ever seen it but me, I see it. I've got a baby boy over at my place that you haven't even bothered to see.

SALLY. Another one?

CLAY. Damn right, another one.

SALLY. I'll stop by. Clay, don't upset him anymore.

CLAY. Don't put on this act with me. You don't care about him. Why don't you go on home? Go back where you came from. We don't need you around. I'll stay with him.

SALLY. Hold it just a goddamn second. You son-of-a-bitch. Now, I can choose to leave this house or not, and that's my business.

CLAY. Yeah? Well, you fucked up so I ain't lending you the money. I won't loan you a penny ...

SALLY. You lousy fuck ... you promised Jack, you promised me!

CLAY. I didn't get my half of the bargain. I wash my hands of the whole mess.

(CLAY exits. SALLY is silent. SHE pours herself another drink.)

GORDON. *(Sadly.)* Clay might know a lot more about Maude's situation than he's telling.

SALLY. He doesn't know anymore than we do, Dad.

GORDON. What was you needing to borrow money from Clay for?

SALLY. Me—borrow money?

GORDON. That's what I heard. He said, "... I ain't lending you the money."

SALLY. That's not what he said.

GORDON. I thought you had all the money you needed.

SALLY. I do.

GORDON. Sell one of them mink coats you've got if you need money. How bad are you in debt?

SALLY. I'm not.

GORDON. Well, what do you need money for?

SALLY. For Jack ... I need it for Jack ... yeah. Jack needed to borrow some money from Clay but he couldn't wait to get it from him—so he asked me to pick it up and drop it off for him on my way home.

GORDON. That don't make a lick of sense ...

SALLY. It don't?

GORDON. I think you been lying to your old man.

SALLY. Why would I lie?

GORDON. I couldn't answer that one. You kids never cared too much for me. But, it might be I'm all you got left!

SALLY. Daddy ... I ... (*SALLY loses all control. SHE puts her face in her hands and weeps. There is a long pause.*)

GORDON. A fellow don't drink that much if he's happy as you said you was.

SALLY. I'm all messed up. The magazine laid me off.

GORDON. *Newsweek*?

SALLY. I never worked for *Newsweek*.

GORDON. You didn't? Who do you work for?

SALLY. I don't work for anybody anymore.

GORDON. You can get another job.

SALLY. I can't even pay my rent. (*Pause.*) Dad, I was trying to recoup my losses but the deal isn't working out like I planned.

GORDON. Can't that husband help you?

SALLY. He's the reason I can't pay my rent. He took every last cent I have and some I don't have and left me for another woman.

GORDON. Tarnation.

SALLY. Then she took everything from him and left him.

GORDON. Smart woman.

SALLY. And now he wants to come back to me.

GORDON. I knew he was worthless as soon as I saw that earring.

SALLY. The only thing I own is that car outside and it's a pile of junk.

GORDON. Sell it.

SALLY. And then my cat died.

GORDON. I can find you any number of cats in the country.

SALLY. Can you just go out and get another horse like Peanuts?

GORDON. I was looking through the ads in the paper just a moment ago. I'll have to find Maude another pony. She'd be lost without a horse to pet. (*Pause.*) So you needed this money to pay your bills in New York?

SALLY. No. That's not the worst of it.

GORDON. Well, you best tell it.

SALLY. I owe some very mean people a lot of money. If I don't have the money in Austin by midnight tonight, they'll collect their way, with interest.

GORDON. You're saying they're dangerous?

SALLY. Their last invoice had the promise of a broken nose attached to it.

GORDON. Dad burn.

SALLY. I'm scared to death.

GORDON. What sort of thing did you buy from them?

SALLY. *I* didn't buy it, Don did.

GORDON. What did Don buy?

SALLY. I don't care to say.

GORDON. Something illegal?

SALLY. Yes.

GORDON. Marijuana?

SALLY. Yes.

GORDON. I smoked me one of those marijuana cigarettes one time. It made me feel like I had a swallow of that Jack Daniels. Ain't that how it makes you feel?

SALLY. Something similar ...

GORDON. Well, land sakes alive, Sally. How come you to get mixed up in a thing like that?

SALLY. I don't know. I really don't. Don made this New York/Texas run a bunch of times.

GORDON. And you knew what he was doing?

SALLY. I guess I knew. But when he split with all the money, he left me ten kilos of grass and a mixed assortment of pills. I just sat with it for a long time. Then these Austin people called asking about their payment and I started getting scared.

GORDON. You're a real puzzle to me, gal.

SALLY. Daddy ... I tried returning the stuff but they wouldn't take it back. Then I got the bright idea to sell it myself. I found someone to buy the kilos, but they ripped me off. Now, I have no grass, no money, nothing.

GORDON. How much do you owe them?

SALLY. Three thousand dollars.

GORDON. Are you hooked up on drugs?

SALLY. Dad ...

GORDON. Now cut the horse shit and tell me the truth.

SALLY. I guess I am.

GORDON. Lordy, lordy ... no wonder things don't sound right.

SALLY. I can't stop taking the pills.

GORDON. They could send you to jail for something like this.

SALLY. I would have come back here as soon as I took care of things.

GORDON. I feel as helpless as a newborn kitten. My women in trouble and here I am, plumb wore out. (*GORDON exits.*)

SALLY. Shit! (*SALLY begins to pace and slowly the tears of rage and hopelessness come. SHE places her hands on the sides of her head and pulls her hair and butts her head into the wall. SHE goes to the phone, dials.)* Ramon, please? This is Sally Pound. *(Pause.)* O.K. He knows where I am. *(SALLY hangs up the phone and sits with it in her lap.)* Shit! *(A long pause. The PHONE rings. SALLY answers it on the first ring.)* Ramon? No. Mother? My mother? Thank God, oh, Mother, we were so worried ... *(Pause.)* We heard the news and it scared us to death. Are you alright?

(A GUNSHOT rings out from Gordon's bedroom. SALLY is stunned. Her hand goes to her heart. SHE stumbles, nearly falling, and breathes erratically.)

SALLY. I'm sorry ... Mother ... a gunshot?... I didn't hear it. Must have been on your end of the phone. Maybe it was a car in the street. Talk to Dad? Well, I think he's asleep right now. I'll have to wake him up.

(The front door opens. CLAY enters.)

CLAY. Did I hear a gunshot?
SALLY. Clay, get Dad, will you?
CLAY. I could have sworn I heard a gunshot.
SALLY. Maybe the neighbor's hunting ... *(On the phone.)* Mother ... I'm getting him now ... but he might have walked out into the pasture.
CLAY. That's Mother?
SALLY. Yes! And she's fine! It wasn't her group that was kidnapped! Now will you please get Dad!
CLAY. Thank God. *(Calling.)* Dad!

SALLY. (*Covering the mouthpiece.*) He might not be able to hear you, Clay ... would you go get him? (*Into the phone.*) He's coming in just a second.

CLAY.(*Yelling.*) Dad! Come on out here ... Mother's on the phone.

SALLY. (*Desperate.*) Clay, for Christ's sake, will you just go back there and see what's going on ... please.

CLAY. Well, for crying out loud! Has he passed out?

(CLAY exits to the bedroom. SALLY speaks on the phone.)

SALLY. You were swimming in The Dead Sea? How exciting ... Jack is great ... we're all just great!

(FOOTSTEPS are heard through the hallway, SALLY waits tensely as GORDON enters shaking his head sheepishly followed by CLAY. SALLY falls to her knees.)

SALLY. Sweet Jesus!
GORDON. What are you doing, Sally?
SALLY. (*Hands him the phone.*) Mother is on the phone.
GORDON. Maude? (*Taking the phone.*) Maude? What in the dickens? Are you alright? Well, you about give me a heart attack. I'm not feeling any too good as it is. Well, turn around and come home! (*Pause.*) Alright, then stay there but I don't like it one bit. (*Pause.*) Yeah. It's been a surprise. She's been here all day. Oh, dern, you can tell her yourself.

(GORDON hands the phone to SALLY. SHE stares at her father in absolute disbelief.)

SALLY. *(Whispering.)* You shit!

GORDON. Your mother wants to talk to you.

SALLY. Hi, again! *(Pause.)* Thanks, Mom. Yeah. Thirty-five years old today! A present for me? How about that? In your desk? Thanks, Mom. *(Pause.)* I promise. *(For Gordon's benefit.)* Now ... you stay close to the preacher. Clay will stay with Dad until you get home. We're taking very good care of him. *(Pause.)* Oh, Don's great, Mother. Just great. Thank you, Mother. *(Pause.)* I love you, too. *(SALLY hands the phone to Gordon.)* Say goodbye.

GORDON. I'll be dern if I can talk right. *(On the phone.)* Yeah. Hi, sweetcakes. Yeah. No. I'm eating real good. I love you, too. Maude? When you get home, things are going to be different around here. I ain't going to be so moody. I'm going to be a new person. I know I've been awful crusty around the edges and I want to apologize. No. No, now I intend to make it up to you. I do. Because, I love you and I don't rightly know what I'd do without you. But the next time you want to see some country other than this farm, I'm going with you. I ain't going to let you leave me with these dern kids again. *(Pause.)* I'm thinking about you, too. Goodbye. *(GORDON hangs up the phone.)* Don't that take the cake. *(Pause.)* I have to take an aspirin, I believe I've got me a headache. *(GORDON exits.)*

CLAY. Mother didn't even ask to speak to me.

SALLY. She sees you all the time, Clay.

CLAY. It's as if she knows what's happening without me telling her. She's disappointed but she won't say it.

SALLY. Disappointed in who?

CLAY. All the years you do good don't make any difference when you hit a bad one.

SALLY. Disappointed in Dad?

CLAY. Too many barns, too many cars ... too much farm equipment ...

SALLY. Disappointed in me?

CLAY. Not you! Me. I'm talking about me. Is that so hard for you to believe? That someone besides you would be the subject?

SALLY. I'm sorry, Clay. I'm so preoccupied, I know I am. But, now that Mother's safe, now we know that she's all right ... could you lend me the money? I could still get to Austin on time. And Dad's fine. It's all O.K. Look, I wouldn't have gotten him drunk but he was so depressed, Clay. Talking suicide ... you don't know what it was like.

CLAY. *I* know. You're the one that doesn't know.

SALLY. I'm going to stick closer, Clay. I promise. I even like the man, isn't that wild?

CLAY. (*Sadly.*) It's not so wild.

(*Pause.*)

SALLY. Clay, I've got to get moving.

(*Pause.*)

CLAY. It appears that I'm up a creek.

SALLY. Up a creek?

CLAY. Sally, I tried to raise your money at the auction ... tried to sell my bull.

SALLY. (*Astounded.*) Cyrano? You tried to sell Cyrano?

CLAY. He should bring six thousand on a bad day but I couldn't even sell him at two.

SALLY. I didn't think you'd have to sell Cyrano, Clay.

CLAY That's what I'm telling you. I couldn't sell the damn bull at any price. Nobody is going to buy from me now, knowing what they know. All they have to do is wait until the bank forecloses. Then they can go to the auction block and get anything I own for next to nothing.

SALLY. Are you telling me you can't lend me the money?

CLAY. I gambled on a large piece of land. Bought it dirt cheap thinking prices were going to go back up ... I couldn't unload it until it was too late. I may lose most of my stock, my farm, the whole shebang. (*A long pause. CLAY breaks down. All is very quiet.*) All the managing and scheming ... none of it worked. Sometimes, I get to feeling so sad I just go hide out in the woods ... I'm so ashamed. (*Pause.*) Billy come up on me the other day and caught me crying. I was damn embarrassed—he was too. (*Pause.*) Connie thinks everything is just fine as long as we can get to the damn church once a week and she can spend an hour at the beauty parlor now and then. Sometimes, I think she's just dumb. I think that's why I married her—because she was the opposite of you.

SALLY. You think I'm smart?

CLAY. I wouldn't go so far as to say that. (*Pause.*) I lost a calf this afternoon, while I was in town. It belonged to Billy. I gave it to him when he was the same age I was when Dad gave me my first calf. Billy left it locked in the pen all night. The little devil broke his neck trying to jump the fence to suck his mother. Well, Billy's only nine, he's too young to expect him not to forget things.

(*Pause.*) Then, I think, maybe he forgot that calf on purpose ... because he caught me crying ... he didn't care about it anymore. (*Pause.*) And, every time I look at you I just get pissed off. They never see you, so all they do is talk about you.

SALLY. I'm sorry. Clay ... I wish there was something ... (*Pause.*) What am I going to do?

CLAY. Jack, he thought I had money. I haven't told him. Haven't told anybody. Not Mother or Dad. It's just you, you're the only one that knows.

SALLY. I've got some serious thinking to do.

CLAY. You're into something ... what is it—illegal?

SALLY. Yep.

CLAY. Could you hide out here?

SALLY. No. I'm a bonafide self destruction freak, Clay. They've got every number in the book. (*Pause.*) Clay?

CLAY. Yeah.

SALLY. What are you going to do?

CLAY. I don't know. Something ... What about you?

SALLY. Oh, stay off the highway.

(CLAY exits.
SALLY goes to the desk, opens it and removes her birthday present from her mother. SHE unwraps it. It is a framed picture.)

SALLY. Oh, Mama ...

(GORDON enters carrying the gun. SALLY sees him, SHE is furious.)

SALLY. What was the gunshot?

GORDON. The what?

SALLY. You son-of-a-bitch. That gunshot I heard. Why didn't you answer Clay when he called you?

GORDON. I was cleaning my pistol and this dern gun went off with me barely touching the trigger.

SALLY. You scared the shit out of me, Dad.

GORDON. I forgot I loaded it. Made me deaf a second. I couldn't hear a thing.

(SALLY breaks into tears.)

GORDON. Well, lord-a-mercy, Sally, what's wrong?

SALLY. What's wrong? What's wrong? You've put me in total shock.

GORDON. I never seen the like.

SALLY. And Mother, she loves me so much. She thinks I'm so wonderful.

GORDON. Of course she does.

SALLY. You took such a wonderful picture.

GORDON. Oh, that, it was her idea.

SALLY. It's beautiful.

GORDON. I've been thinking, I've always wanted to see the State Capital of Texas.

SALLY. What?

GORDON. I've never been there. We could take us a ride down there. Go sightseeing ... and I'd help you tend to that business of yours. I'll take my pistol if they give us any trouble. That's why I was cleaning it.

SALLY. I don't want to get you mixed up in this.

GORDON. I reckon that banker is still at that sale. He'd give me my money. If you promise me couple of things, I'll help you pay those fellers what you owe them.

SALLY. I can promise you one thing. I'm getting myself off drugs. When I heard your gun go off, I thought I was going to have a heart attack. I could feel my heart jumping around in there—missing beats. And I thought, if I don't quit taking speed, I'm going to drop dead.

GORDON. Well, now old Doc Reed is just a horse doctor but he might be able to help you get started not taking those pills.

SALLY. I'm afraid.

GORDON. Ain't nothing wrong with being a little scared. Makes you cautious about walking into traps. But, you can't be too scared to get out of a trap once you get caught. You'd wind up spending the rest of your life there. Now, I wouldn't mind taking a look at what they got left at that cow sale ... buy you a calf for your birthday ...

SALLY. There's something I need.

GORDON. That way, when you ain't here, I can go out and talk to the calf.

SALLY. Gordon Pound, the miser of East Texas, is going to spend money?

GORDON. Dern right. Ain't got much but I've a mind to buy me a pet calf and lend some of it to you. I never was too much help to you kids. Better do it now if I'm going to do it. Besides, if I didn't help you get clear of this and Maude found out, she'd whup me worse than you did. You'll have to pay me back when you get squared away.

SALLY. Clay just told me that he's bankrupt.

GORDON. Clay will take care of himself. He always has. Probably wouldn't take any help if I was to offer it.

Don't start arguing with me, now, I'm old and I ain't got that much time left.

SALLY. That's bullshit, Dad.

GORDON. We could drive to Austin, pay them fellers, see the capital and eat us some Chinese food ... I always wanted to eat in one of those Chinese restaurants. I only ask one thing in return.

SALLY. I'm listening.

GORDON. If it ever comes down to it, I want you to pull the plug on me.

SALLY. Pull the plug?

GORDON. If I was to get laid up in the hospital with machines pumping my blood for me and tubes feeding me, I would want you to pull the plug.

SALLY. Are you serious?

GORDON. Dern right, I'm serious. When my own brother died, there wasn't a tear shed at his funeral. And it wasn't because he wasn't a good man, they was just tired of dealing with him. He was mean. I can't say I blame them, but, still, it's sad, I believe. A man's own kin looking forward to his funeral. I don't want to lie in a hospital bed for a year with a bunch of people staring over me, waiting and hoping I'll get on with it and die. But, I ask you, what's my alternative? Clay ain't going to upset Maude, and she ain't got the heart for it, and Jack, he can't be counted on in times of stress ... I want you to make sure it was done.

SALLY. Sweet Jesus ...

GORDON. I think he would approve.

SALLY. You do?

GORDON. Yep.

SALLY. Alright. I'll pull the plug.

GORDON. Thank you.

SALLY. Don't mention it. (*Pause.*) I'm going to do better, Dad.

GORDON. Good. 'Cause if something happens to Maude, I'm coming to live with you.

SALLY. Oh, my God.

GORDON. And promise me you won't have nothing to do with that dern worthless excuse for a husband.

SALLY. I promise.

GORDON. And, whatever happens, promise you won't leave me with dern Clay.

SALLY. You're demanding a lot, aren't you?

GORDON. I'm paying for the gas.

SALLY. That's right.

GORDON. Well, I'll die some day, but not today. (*Pause.*) Get the car keys and let's go buy something living. If she can spend thousands of dollars risking her life in the Holy Land I can buy me some kind of animal. Then, we'll go play cops and robbers.

SALLY. For the first and last time.

GORDON. I always did want to ride shotgun.

SALLY. Remarkable person ...

GORDON. Well ...

(GORDON awkwardly embraces his daughter. There is a pause. The LIGHTS fade as the TWO begin preparing to leave.)

GORDON. And on the way past Clay's house, I want you to stop. I'm going to get back my wire cutters.

THE END

COSTUME PLOT

SALLY
Worn blue jeans
T-shirt

GORDON
Union suit for Act I, Scene 1
Worn overalls
Western shirt
Farmer's cap

CLAY
Worn and soiled blue jeans
Western shirt
Summer cowboy hat
Worn cowboy boots

PROPERTY PLOT

Offstage Pre-set Act I

Ice chest containing 2 beer bottles filled with ginger ale
  with tops screws back on.
Back pack containing:
  Coffee in Jack Daniels bottle. One cup of coffee
  to four cups of water.
  Two pills in film canister
  Ramon's phone number on a slip of paper
  Cut off blue jeans and T-shirt
Shotgun
Vacuum cleaner
Wire cutters
Bowl of corn flakes with milk and spoon (put small
  amount of cereal in bowl with spoon, milk to the side in
  carton.
Glass of water
2 cups of coffee
Small suitcase

Off Stage Pre-set Act II

Dominoes on wooden board
Two tumblers
Two pistols: small one with blanks; one pistol in leather
  case (no blanks)
Cloth to clean gun
"Classified Ads" on prop shelf

On Stage Pre-set Act I

Telephone on desk
Note to Sally in envelope on top of desk
Three pill bottles (top right desk drawer)

(Strike dominoes and board, beer and cup, small suitcase,
    reset back pack and contents.)

On Stage Pre-set Act II
Small electric fan (turn on)
Gift box (wrapped in drawer of desk) containing framed
    photo
Record in Country Western genre album cover
Record player
Photo album and Yearbook

Personal Props—Sally
Set $2.50 in jeans
Almost empty beer bottle and car keys
Two pills in film canister

Personal Props—Gordon
Red bandana (used as handkerchief)
Pocket watch
$3.00 in overall's pocket

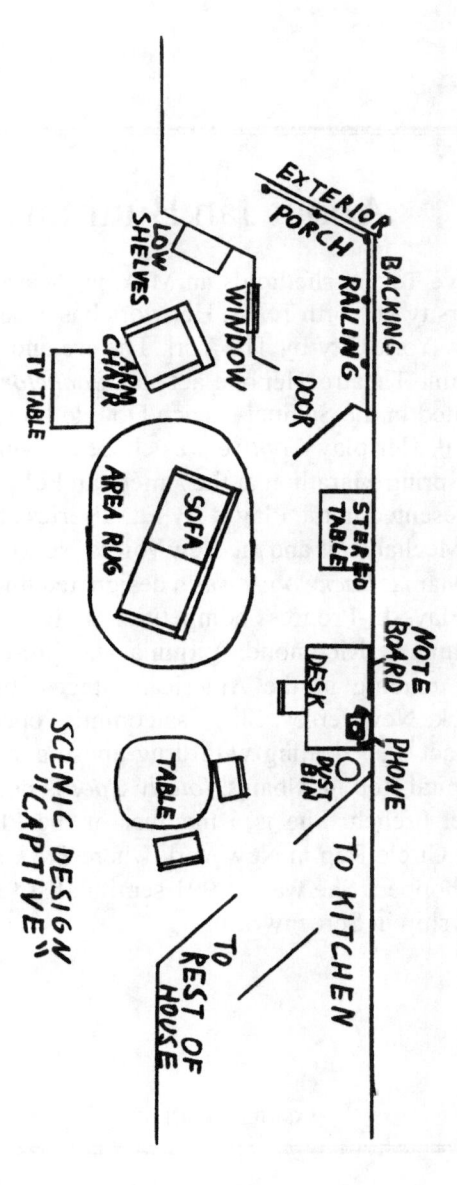

SCENIC DESIGN "CAPTIVE"

About Jan Buttram

A native Texan, she holds an M.A. in theatre from the University of North Texas. Her work has been produced in New York City by The York Theatre and The Pulse Ensemble Theatre. Her one-act play *Bachelor Flats* was presented in the Samuel French/Double Image Theatre Festival. Her play *Captive* was chosen a winner in the 1988 Spring Marathon at the American Folk Theatre, and presented in the Play It By Ear 2 series at The New Rude Mechanicals and the New Voices/New Plays series at La Mama. *Backwoods* was a designated finalist in the New-Plays-In-Progress competition at The Production Company in Richmond, Virginia and presented as a staged reading at the American Stage Company in Teaneck, New Jersey. She was commissioned to write a one-act play dealing with drug abuse and teenagers by Capital Rep in Albany. *Totally Cool* is published by Samuel French. She is a member of the Playwrights Lab at Circle Rep in New York where *Backwoods* was workshopped. She was a 1991 semifinalist for a Nicoll Fellowship in Screenwriting.

OTHER TITLES AVAILABLE FROM SAMUEL FRENCH

SKIN DEEP
Jon Lonoff

Comedy / 2m, 2f / Interior Unit Set

In *Skin Deep*, a large, lovable, lonely-heart, named Maureen Mulligan, gives romance one last shot on a blind-date with sweet awkward Joseph Spinelli; she's learned to pepper her speech with jokes to hide insecurities about her weight and appearance, while he's almost dangerously forthright, saying everything that comes to his mind. They both know they're perfect for each other, and in time they come to admit it.

They were set up on the date by Maureen's sister Sheila and her husband Squire, who are having problems of their own: Sheila undergoes a non-stop series of cosmetic surgeries to hang onto the attractive and much-desired Squire, who may or may not have long ago held designs on Maureen, who introduced him to Sheila. With Maureen particularly vulnerable to both hurting and being hurt, the time is ripe for all these unspoken issues to bubble to the surface.

"Warm-hearted comedy ... the laughter was literally show-stopping. A winning play, with enough good-humored laughs and sentiment to keep you smiling from beginning to end."
– *TalkinBroadway.com*

"It's a little Paddy Chayefsky, a lot Neil Simon and a quick-witted, intelligent voyage into the not-so-tranquil seas of middle-aged love and dating. The dialogue is crackling and hilarious; the plot simple but well-turned; the characters endearing and quirky; and lurking beneath the merriment is so much heartache that you'll stand up and cheer when the unlikely couple makes it to the inevitable final clinch."
– *NYTheatreWorld.Com*

BLUE YONDER
Kate Aspengren

Dramatic Comedy / Monolgues and scenes
12f (can be performed with as few as 4 with doubling) / Unit Set

A familiar adage states, "Men may work from sun to sun, but women's work is never done." In Blue Yonder, the audience meets twelve mesmerizing and eccentric women including a flight instructor, a firefighter, a stuntwoman, a woman who donates body parts, an employment counselor, a professional softball player, a surgical nurse professional baseball player, and a daredevil who plays with dynamite among others. Through the monologues, each woman examines her life's work and explores the career that she has found. Or that has found her.